a Rumpus in the night!

Nick Ward

meadowside
CHILDREN'S BOOKS

Right in the **middle** of a scary monster sort of dream,
Jamie woke up.

He woke up so suddenly
that part of his dream stayed with him,
and crashing into the bedroom came...

...a **Rumpus!**

It was one of the monsters
from Jamie's dream,
and he looked
VERY surprised!

"Help!"

roared Jamie.
"There's a monster in my room."

"Help!"

cried the Rumpus in a snuffly,
gruffly voice.

"There's a horrid,
roaring monster."

Then with a clash and a clatter,
he dived under Jamie's bed.

Jamie was astonished. Surely, hairy little monsters don't get scared, he thought.

"Come out monster, I won't hurt you,"
whispered Jamie, leaning over.

The Rumpus crawled out from under the bed.
"It's dark and I'm frightened and I want to go home," he said.

"You're from my dream," said Jamie.
"How do you get home?"

"You must go back to sleep," snuffled the Rumpus.
"And then I'll pop back into your dream."

"But I'm wide awake now," said Jamie, turning on the light.
"And if I can't get to sleep, Mummy always reads me a story."

"But I can't read," said the Rumpus.

"Then I'll read you a story," said Jamie.
"And then perhaps we'll both fall asleep."

So the Rumpus tried to climb on to Jamie's bed.

"Whoa!" he cried as the covers started to slip.

"Shush Rumpus," whispered Jamie as the monster slid to the floor with a wallop. "You'll wake everyone up!"

"It's not a scary story, is it?" asked a muffled Rumpus from under a tangle of bedclothes. "I don't like scary stories."

Mumf!

Jamie read one story, then another, **then** the first story all over again...
but they were STILL wide awake.

"Sometimes I'm allowed to play a game if I can't sleep," said Jamie.
"Let's play Snakes and Ladders."

BANG!

"Snakes?" squealed the Rumpus.
He jumped into the wardrobe to hide and, with a crash, the nervous monster pulled down a rail of clothes.

"I d-don't like s-snakes," came a muffled voice from underneath a pile of coats.

CRASH!

OOF!

"It's only a game," said Jamie.
"Come out and I'll show you."

"I'M THE WINNER!" roared the Rumpus,
marching around the bedroom in triumph.
"Let's have another go...whoops!"
He tripped over the game and sent it flying through the air.

"Shush," said Jamie. "You'll wake everyone up."

"Sorry," whispered the Rumpus. "Aren't you sleepy yet?"

"Not one little bit," sighed Jamie. "Let's play Tag," he said. "You're it!"

"**You're** the **monster!**" he cried, tagging Jamie.

"**NO**, you're the monster!"

Then Jamie and Rumpus played
...Follow My Leader! They marched,

...and jumped,

...and skipped.

They bounced on Jamie's bed,
and made a right HULLABALOO...

. . . until they were completely puffed out.

"I'm not scared anymore," panted the Rumpus, collapsing in a heap.
"Don't go to sleep yet. I want to play some more."

"But I'm so tired," yawned Jamie, crawling into bed. "I'm so…"

"Wake up, Jamie!" cried the Rumpus.

But Jamie fell fast asleep, and the Rumpus… disappeared

MONSTER BOOK

Far, far away in another world,
a **Rumpus** woke up in the **middle**
of a scary monster sort of dream.
He woke up so **suddenly**
that part of his dream stayed with him,
and **crashing** into his bedroom, came…

…Jamie!

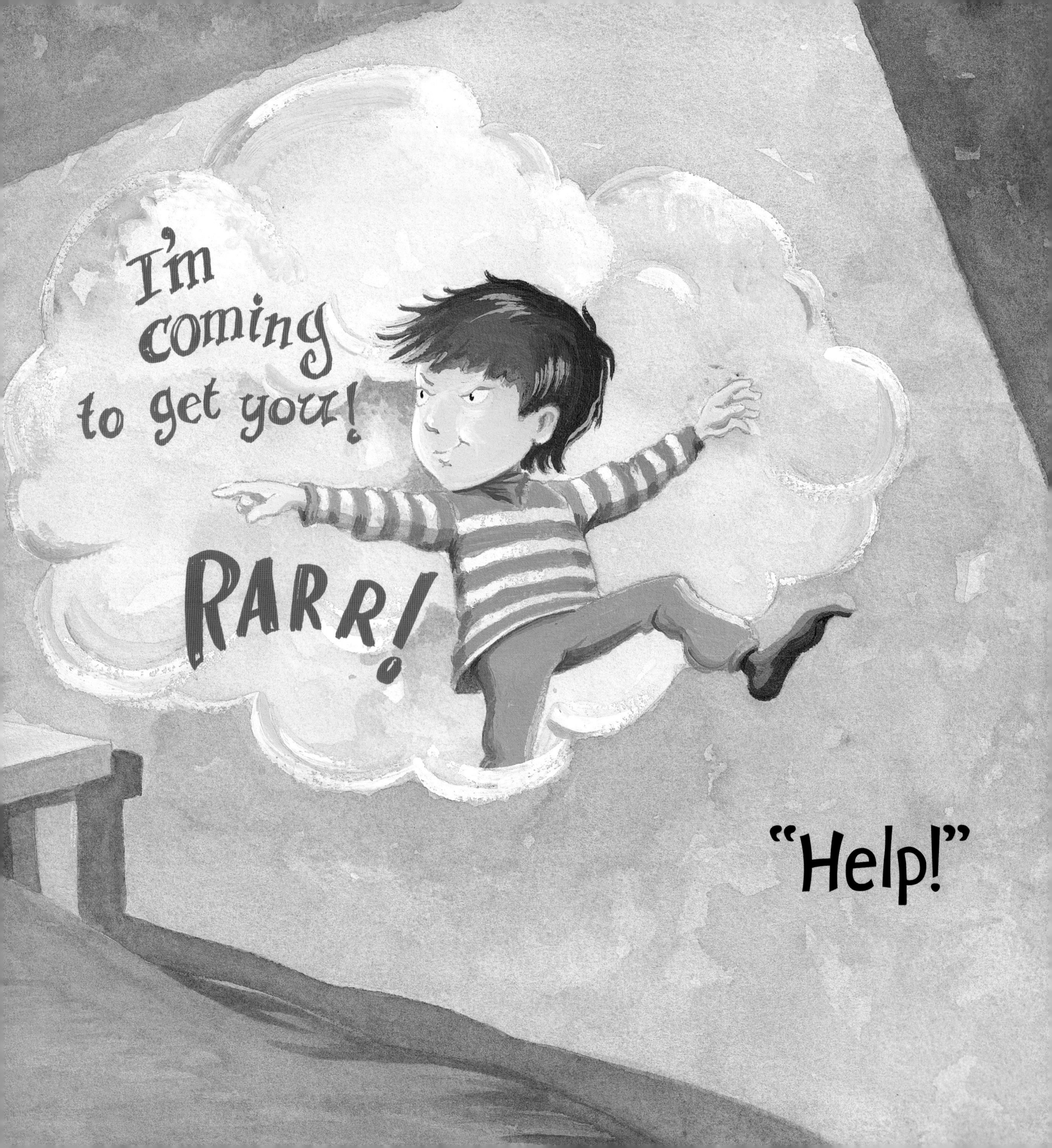

"Help!"

For Jimmy!
N.W.

First published in 2007
by Meadowside Children's Books
185 Fleet Street, London, EC4A 2HS

www.meadowsidebooks.com

Text and illustrations © Nick Ward 2007

The right of Nick Ward to be identified as the
author and illustrator of this work has been
asserted by him in accordance with the
Copyright, Designs and Patents Act, 1988

A CIP catalogue record for this book
is available from the British Library
Printed in China

10 9 8 7 6 5 4 3 2 1